De Colores
BRIGHT WITH COLORS

DE Colores
BRIGHT WITH Colors

pictures by
David Diaz

Marshall Cavendish Children

Illustrations copyright © 2008 by David Diaz
First Marshall Cavendish paperback edition, 2011

Marshall Cavendish Corporation
99 White Plains Road
Tarrytown, NY 10591
www.marshallcavendish.us/kids

Library of Congress Cataloging-in-Publication Data
De colores — Bright with colors / illustrated by David Diaz. — 1st ed.
    p. cm.
  Spanish and English words.
  Includes music score.
  978-0-7614-5431-1 (hardcover) 978-0-7614-5934-7 (paperback)
  1. Children's songs, Spanish. 2. Children's songs, English.
  I. Diaz, David. ill II. Title: Bright with colors.
M1998 .D   782.42'0268—dc22   2007022133

The illustrations were rendered in acrylic, pencil, and colored pencil.
Book design by Vera Soki
Editor: Margery Cuyler

Printed in Malaysia (T)
1 3 5 6 4 2

mc **Marshall Cavendish**
Children

for
Buttercup
D.D.

De colores,
de colores se visten los campos
en la primavera.

De colores,
bright with colors the mountains
and valleys dress up
in the springtime.

De colores,
de colores son los pajaritos que vienen
de afuera.

De colores,
bright with colors all the little birds
fill the skies in the daytime.

De colores,
de colores es el arco iris que
vemos lucir.

De colores,
bright with colors the rainbow brings joy
with the glory of spring.

Y por eso los grandes amores
de muchos colores me gustan
a mí.

And a bright love has found us
with peace all around us
that makes our hearts sing.

Y por eso los grandes amores
de muchos colores me gustan
a mí.

And a bright love has found us
with peace all around us
that makes our hearts sing.

Canta el gallo,
canta el gallo con el *quirí, quirí, quirí, quirí, quirí.*

Sings the rooster,
sings the rooster with his *kiri, kiri, kiri, kiri, kiri.*

La gallina,
la gallina con el cara, cara, cara, cara, cara.

And the cluck hen,
and the cluck hen with her *cara, cara, cara, cara, cara.*

Los polluelos,
los polluelos con el *pío, pío, pío, pío, pí.*

And the baby chicks,
and the baby chicks with their *pío, pío, pío, pío, pí*.

Y por eso los grandes amores
de muchos colores me gustan
a mí.

And a bright love has found us
with peace all around us
that makes our hearts sing.

Composed by a group of pilgrims on the mountain roads of Spain in the sixteenth century, "De colores" is now sung all over the Spanish-speaking world on special occasions. People hold hands and sway as they sing the familiar words. It is also the anthem of the United Farm Workers of America, a union founded by César Chávez in 1962. The version in this book is well-known, but there are other versions that include additional stanzas.

David Diaz won the Caldecott Medal for his illustrations in *Smoky Night* by Eve Bunting and two Pura Belpré Honor Book awards for his illustrations in *César: ¡Sí, se puede! Yes, We Can!* and *Diego: Bigger than Life* by Carmen T. Bernier-Grand. His work has also been featured in national publications such as *The Atlantic Monthly* and *The Washington Post*. He grew up in southern Florida and now lives in Carlsbad, California.